MR. PAPADILLY AND WILLY

MR. PAPADILLY

AND WILLY

BY
FLORENCE & LOUIS SLOBODKIN

VANGUARD PRESS, INC.
NEW YORK NEW YORK

Copyright, ©, 1964, by Florence and Louis Slobodkin

Library of Congress Catalogue Card Number: 64-23322

Published simultaneously in Canada by The Copp, Clark Publishing Co. Limited., Toronto. No portion of this book may be reprinted in any form without the written permission of the publisher, except by a reviewer who may wish to quote brief portions in connection with a review for a newspaper or magazine.

Manufactured in the United States of America

   Mr. Papadilly, a quiet, gentle man, became a Lion Tamer quite by accident.

   A friend who lived far away sent him a Lion Cub. Never having had a Lion Cub before, Mr. Papadilly did not know what to do with him. So he did nothing. He just kept him and fed him and named him Willy.

   Mr. Papadilly grew quite fond of Willy. He never spoke harshly to him because that was not necessary. Willy was gentle, too, and as he grew fond of Mr. Papadilly, he was always obedient and tried to please.

Every day Mr. Papadilly sat on his front porch and watched his neighbors peeking through the fence around his house.

"See the baby lion," they would say to their children. "No, it is not a little dog. It's a lion . . . a gentle baby lion."

Of course, as Willy grew older he grew bigger. And since the neighbors had known him as a baby, they were not afraid of him. They knew he was kindhearted and gentle.

One day a Circus Man came to Mr. Papadilly's house and asked him to sell his lion to the circus.

But Mr. Papadilly said he could not part with him. Willy was a very nice pet, much more interesting than a cat or a dog or a canary.

"Then you come along, too," said the man. "You can be the Lion Tamer in the circus."

"Me . . . a Lion Tamer in the circus!" exclaimed Mr. Papadilly. "That is ridiculous!"

But he could see that Willy liked the idea of being a Circus Lion. So, after a while, Mr. Papadilly said, "All right" and he and Willy joined the circus.

It was in the circus that Mr. Papadilly came to be called Papadilly. His name was really Mr. Ernest Dilly. But the circus people always spoke of him as Papa Dilly because he was like a papa or daddy to Willy. Soon people thought of him only as Papadilly. Nobody remembered that he was really Mr. Ernest Dilly.

And the same thing happened to Willy, the lion. At first everyone in the circus called him Mr. Dilly's Willy, but soon people forgot why they were calling the lion Mr. Dilly's Willy and he was known only as Dillywilly.

When the Ringmaster announced their circus act he always shouted, "And now here are Dillywilly, the Most Ferocious Lion in the World, and Mr. Papadilly, the Bravest and Most Courageous Lion Tamer."

Everyone who saw Mr. Papadilly perform agreed that he was surely the Bravest and Most Courageous Lion Tamer that ever was.

Of course, Dillywilly really needed no taming. Mr. Papadilly only had to whisper to him to do something and he did it.

"Jump through this hoop," whispered Mr. Papadilly. Then he jumped aside quickly as though he were terribly afraid of this Ferocious Lion.

Dillywilly jumped through the hoop. People clapped their hands and Mr. Papadilly bowed to their applause.

"Run around the arena," whispered Mr. Papadilly and cracked his whip fiercely (though he was very careful never to touch Dillywilly with it).

Dillywilly ran around the arena. The audience stood up, waved their hats in the air, and shouted, "Bravo! Hooray!"

Mr. Papadilly whispered to Dillywilly, "Go out . . . back to our own tent," and he snapped his whip again, loudly and fiercely.

Dillywilly ran out of the arena and Mr. Papadilly bowed and smiled at the audience.

Dillywilly was very happy in the circus and so was Mr. Papadilly . . . or so it seemed . . . until one day.

Mr. Papadilly watched the throngs of people leaving the circus after the performance.

"All those people," he said to the Clown who stood beside him, "are going home to their little houses."

"It must be nice to live in a house," said the Clown wistfully. "In summer you talk to your neighbors over the back fence. In winter you sit by the fire with a good book."

Later Mr. Papadilly thought about that.

And the next day and the day after that he thought about it ... about a little house where he could again talk to neighbors over a fence in the summer and sit by a roaring fire with a good book in the winter ... with Dillywilly curled up beside him.

"The circus is fine," he said to himself. "But I've worked long enough, and it's time Willy and I lived a nice, quiet, normal life ... in a little house instead of in a tent ... where I can read and think ... leisurely."

And Mr. Papadilly decided to leave the circus!

When he told the circus people, the Manager said, "Please don't leave now. The Papadilly-Dillywilly Act is becoming famous. People come to the circus just to see your act."

But Mr. Papadilly was determined to leave.

So the circus people made a farewell party, and as a farewell present they gave him a little statue of a Roman gladiator and a lion.

On the statue was written:

      MR. PAPADILLY AND DILLYWILLY

Mr. Papadilly shook hands with everyone, and he and Dillywilly and the statue left in the new station wagon Mr. Papadilly had bought.

As soon as they left the circus, Mr. Papadilly said, "Now we will be called by our real names . . . no more of this silly Papadilly and Dillywilly. I am Mr. Ernest Dilly and you are Willy."

And that was what they called themselves. But nobody else called them by those names . . . or by any other names, because there was nobody around who knew them or called them anything at all.

They went directly to the new little house that Mr. Papadilly had rented. It had a nice back yard where Dillywilly could run and play to his heart's content. And he did . . . for just two days . . . because it rained and nobody else was out.

But when the sun came out, the neighbors did, too. And when they saw Dillywilly running around the back yard, they snatched up their children and rushed to their homes.

"A Lion!" they cried to one another. "There's a Lion in that yard!"

They bolted their doors and shut their windows . . . as if Dillywilly would follow them!

In vain did Mr. Papadilly call after them, "Don't be afraid! He's as gentle as a kitten."

But the neighbors did not listen. After they bolted their doors and windows they telephoned the police. In a little while a policeman came to Mr. Papadilly's house and said:

"You cannot keep a Lion here! We must take him away!"

"Oh, no," cried Mr. Papadilly. "He's my pet. I won't give him up. I'll move away with him . . . this very day."

Mr. Papadilly remembered a little house way off in the woods that belonged to the friend who had given him Dillywilly in the first place. While the policeman waited, Mr. Papadilly telephoned.

His friend said he would not be using his little house for a long time so Mr. Papadilly could go there.

Mr. Papadilly was delighted!

He and Dillywilly got into the station wagon and away they went.

They rode for a long time . . . through highways and byways. They rode through narrow country roads and twisted lanes.

And at last they came to the little house in the woods.

As Mr. Papadilly let Dillywilly out of the station wagon he said, "Now nobody will be afraid of you. No one lives here but the wood animals. Now we can settle down to a peaceful, normal life of leisure."

But that was easier said than done.

Again, for a while, everything was fine. Dillywilly ran around the woods freely and happily. At night he came home and sat cozily in front of the fire with Mr. Papadilly, who read a good book . . . about a circus.

One morning when Dillywilly was out playing somewhere in the woods, Mr. Papadilly heard a terrific noise.

"That was a shot!" he cried and ran out of the house. Then he thought, "There are hunters about! They must be shooting at Willy!"

Fortunately, just then he saw Dillywilly. He, too, had been frightened by the noise of the shot and was rushing home.

Mr. Papadilly did not waste a minute. Quickly he let Dillywilly into the house and bolted the door. And he would not let him out of the house the rest of that day or the next day or the next, for fear of the hunters.

But Mr. Papadilly was a sensible man and he knew that he could not keep Dillywilly cooped up much longer.

"Nobody can stay indoors forever," he said to himself. "Especially a lion. I must think of someplace we can go where Willy will be safe and happy."

He thought and thought. Finally he had an idea.

"We will travel! We'll be a Private Circus and do our act on the road. And someday in our travels we'll find a place where we can settle down to a quiet, normal, leisurely life."

So they got into the station wagon and started on their travels.

After a while they came to a town. There they stopped. Mr.

Papadilly painted a sign and put it beside the station wagon. The sign said:

Mr. Ernest Dilly, Lion Tamer

and

Willy, the Lion

Will Perform This Afternoon

COME ONE! COME ALL!

Many people passed the wagon and read the sign, and Mr. Papadilly said to Dillywilly, "We will have a large audience this afternoon."

But that afternoon only a few children came to see the show. Then an old man came along, stopped for a minute, and went on.

Mr. Papadilly whispered to Dillywilly to go back into the wagon while he ran after the old man.

"Sir," said Mr. Papadilly, "may I ask you a question?"

The old man took the pipe out of his mouth and nodded. Quickly Mr. Papadilly asked his question.

"Don't people in this town like circus acts? Why have they not come to see my act?"

"Because," said the old man, "yours is just a little act. Nobody has ever heard of you. But on the other side of town there is a real circus with a Really Ferocious Lion and a Most Courageous Lion Tamer. You must have heard of them. They are world-famous.... They are Mr. Papadilly and Dillywilly!"

"Oh-oh," said Mr. Papadilly.

He thanked the old man and went back to the station wagon where Dillywilly waited.

"Willy," he said, "we are world-famous, and somebody is using our act and our names. We must look into this!"

He drove to the other end of town to the circus. Leaving Dillywilly in the station wagon, Mr. Papadilly went to the Circus Manager's tent.

The Manager was very happy to see him.

"How we've missed you!" he cried. "I suppose you've heard . . . . We had to hire another man with a lion and call them Papadilly and Dillywilly. But their act is really not very good . . . not half as good as yours."

"What right has anyone to use my name and my act?" asked Mr. Papadilly indignantly.

"It had to be done because people came to the circus especially to see your act. But I'm afraid they won't be coming much longer."

The Manager sounded very sad as he continued.

"The word will soon get around that the Papadilly-Dillywilly Act is not as good as it used to be . . . unless . . . unless you . . ."

Suddenly a Clown's head appeared through the flap of the Circus Manager's tent.

"There's an animal loose!" cried the Clown.

The Manager grabbed his megaphone and ran out with Mr. Papadilly close behind. They followed the Clown and the crowd of people, who were all moving in one direction.

Soon they came to the scene of the excitement.

A large crowd was gathered around Mr. Papadilly's station wagon, and huddled against a corner outside the wagon was Dillywilly!

"Stand back!" "This is the Most Ferocious Lion in the World!" "Look at his eyes!" "Children, stand back!"

People were shouting warnings to one another, yet crowding as closely as they dared around Dillywilly.

Mr. Papadilly could see at a glance that poor Dillywilly was frightened by having so many people so close to him. He could perform at the circus, where he was a safe distance from the crowd. But here were hundreds of people only a few feet away!

As Mr. Papadilly ran forward to lead Dillywilly back into the wagon, the Circus Manager raised his megaphone and spoke to the people.

"Ladies and gentlemen," he said, "we have here none other than the Ferocious Lion, Dillywilly, who, as you can see, is quietly and slyly preparing to pounce upon you. But be calm, ladies and gentlemen, because fortunately the Bravest, Most Courageous Lion Tamer in the Whole Wide World is here, too.

"In his inimitable, mysterious way, Mr. Papadilly will lead the lion into the wagon. There the Ferocious Beast will growl angrily because he will be deprived of his prey . . . you . . . whom he would devour were it not for the amazing Mr. Papadilly!"

The people in the crowd seemed to stop breathing. They watched open-mouthed as Mr. Papadilly stuck out his chest and with firm, brave steps walked up close to Dillywilly.

He waved his hands high in the air as though he were brandishing a whip (which unfortunately he did not have with him at the moment) and whispered to Dillywilly:

"Go into the wagon," he said in a voice so low that even the people just a few feet away could not hear him. "And growl . . . loudly . . . and roar . . . ferociously!"

Dillywilly was very happy to run into the wagon away from all those excited people. Quickly the Circus Manager locked the door of the wagon, as if to keep Dillywilly from coming out again.

Then he spoke through his megaphone . . . very loudly, because Dillywilly's growling and roaring were so loud and so frightening!

"Now we are safe!" shouted the Circus Manager.

"Hooray, hooray!" cried the people. "He saved our lives. What courage! What bravery!"

They pushed and shoved as they all tried to get close to Mr. Papadilly. Those who could reach him shook his hands and slapped him on the back. And all the while they praised him and marveled at his courage.

It was a long time before the crowd went away.

At last Mr. Papadilly and the Circus Manager were left alone . . . with Dillywilly waiting in the wagon.

"I was about to beg you," said the Manager, "to please . . . please tell Dillywilly to stop roaring so we can talk."

Of course, Dillywilly was very glad to stop roaring and growling when Mr. Papadilly told him to.

"Now," said the Circus Manager, "I was about to say . . . please come back to the circus!"

Mr. Papadilly looked into the wagon, and it seemed to him that Dillywilly looked happier now than he had for a long time. And suddenly Mr. Papadilly realized that Dillywilly had been bored.

"He needs to work," he thought. "And his work is here in the circus. Besides, here no hunters will shoot him and no neighbors will run away. Here Dillywilly will be honored and happy and safe. As for me . . . I must admit that without work I, too, was bored. Instead of reading a book about a circus, I will be happier working in the circus."

The Circus Manager interrupted his thoughts.

"Well, Mr. Papadilly," he said, "will you come back to the circus?"

"Yes," said Mr. Papadilly. Then he laughed.

"What are you laughing at?" asked the Manager.

"Oh, nothing . . . really," said Mr. Papadilly.

How could he tell the Circus Manager that he laughed because he was so happy to hear himself called Mr. Papadilly again, and he was so happy to come back to the Circus where he and Dillywilly would again be

DILLYWILLY, THE MOST FEROCIOUS LION ALIVE

AND

MR. PAPADILLY, THE BRAVEST AND MOST COURAGEOUS LION TAMER IN THE WHOLE WIDE WORLD